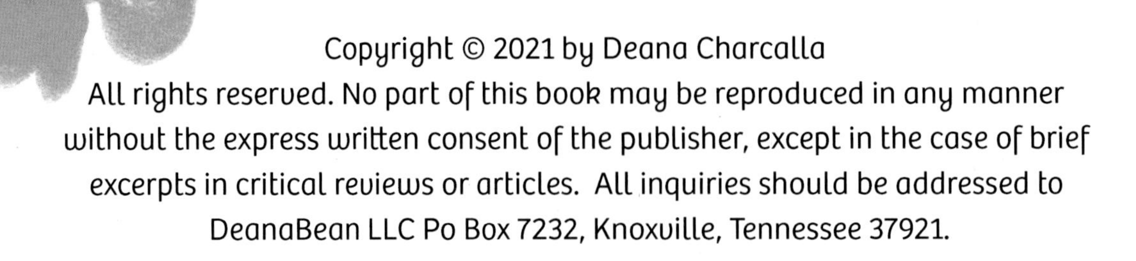

DeanaBean LLC books may be purchased in bulk at special discounts for sales promotion, corporate gift, fund-raising, or educational purposes. Special editions can also be created to specifications. For details, contact Deana Charcalla at
DeanaBean.com or
DeanaBeanbooks@gmail.com

Written By Deana Charcalla
Illustrations By Design By Darlee Orcullo Urbiztondo

Print ISBN: 978-1-7376318-6-6

First Edition

Keep in touch!
You can find us at DeanaBean.com or
DeanaBeanbooks@gmail.com

Published in the United States of America by
DeanaBean LLC

PRINTED IN THE UNITED STATES OF AMERICA
10 9 8 7 6 5 4 3 2 1

Dedicated to:

Judah, Elias, Joseph, Gavin, Miles, Sammy and all
the little ones out there that love the Dinosaur books.
This ones for you guys.

YIKES!!!
DINOSAUR'S
ARE TAKING
OVER THE
BACKYARD!
Dino-Toys

This book belongs to

Dino-Toys

"Mom, we're going outside to play," said Judah. He grabbed one side of the big box he and his little brother Eli had packed and headed out the backdoor. It was filled to the top with their dinosaurs.

"Boys! Stay where I can see you. Don't leave the yard," said their mother, who was cooking at the counter, as their little sister Eden napped.

Eli giggled, "We never need to leave the yard because all the fun comes to us, Mom."
Their Mom put her hands on her hips and shook her head.

Judah said, "Don't worry Mom. I promise we won't leave the yard."

Judah grabbed his favorite Tyrannosaurus Rex that he named TT Rex. Eli picked up the Triceratops.

They ran for the swings, both holding their favorite dino. Eli swung on his belly pretending to fly. Judah kicked his legs out, swinging high.

BANG! The boys saw a big foot **GROWING, GROWING, GROWING! OUT OF THE TOYS.**

"Oh no Eli! Mom will not like this. Our dinos are coming to life," said Judah.

Then Eli yelled, **"YIKES! DINOSAURS ARE TAKING OVER THE BACKYARD!"**

POP!
Dino Toys

"THAT'S ONE BIG FOOT!" said Eli.

"Oh no Eli! Mom will not like this. A Brontosaurus is so big. What if it knocks down the house?" said Judah.

Eli jumped as another large foot shot up at him. They watched as the Brontosaurus grew taller and looked down at them. He looked up and yelled, "Hi dino! What's your name?"

Its gigantic head swung down, looking the kids right in the eyes. "Hello! My name is Diamond. Can't you tell from my sparkling skin."

The boys shook their heads yes. Diamond did look like an enormous, blue, glittering, Brontosaurus to them.

"Nice to meet you Diamond. I'm Judah and this is Eli, my little brother."

"Sorry, we thought you were going to step on us with your big feet," said Eli.

Dino Toys

"I don't step on little boys with my feet," said Diamond.

"Eli, did you know that Brontosaurus means **THUNDER LIZARD?**"

"Really? That's funny Judah. The only thing I know is that they are herbivores," said Eli.

"Paleontologists believe they could have lived to be over 100 years old," said Judah

"Diamond. Are you 100 years old?" asked Eli

"No Eli, I'm 7 years old, and you should pronounce brontosaurus, BRONT-uh-SAWR-us."

Eli giggled, "I'm sorry Diamond. I didn't mean to mispronounce your name."

"That's okay Eli, you're still young," said Diamond

CRASH! They saw Judah's Tyrannosaurus Rex **GROWING, GROWING, GROWING!** out of the toys.

Eli yelled, **"YIKES! DINOSAURS ARE TAKING OVER THE BACKYARD!"**

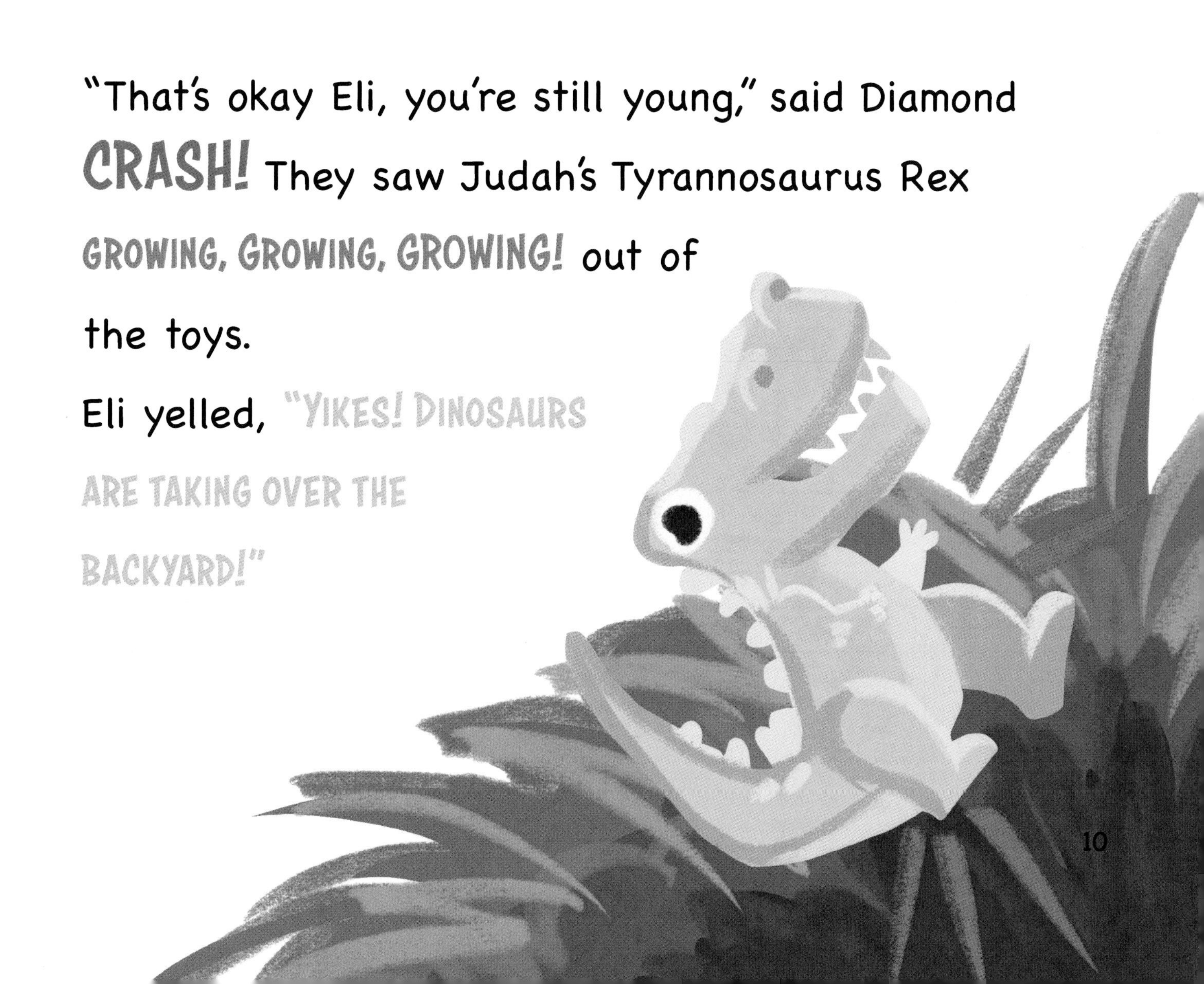

"THAT'S A LOT OF
POINTY TEETH!"
SAID ELI.

"Oh no Eli! Mom will not like this. A Tyrannosaurus Rex is large. What if it gets out of the backyard and destroys the whole neighborhood?" said Judah.

"Wow! That is one big TT Rex," said Eli, watching as the Tyrannosaurus Rex grew to be 42 feet long. Then he yelled, "Hi dino! What's your name?"

Judah looked at him, "Eli! He's going to eat us now."

"We don't know that, he may be a vegetarian," Eli giggled.

"Roar!" said the dino, looking at them.

"I don't think he's a vegetarian, Eli."

"Roar! Roar!" said the dino.

Both boys screamed, "Run for your life!"

"Why are you hiding? I thought you wanted to know my name."

The Tyrannosaurus Rex said, "My name is Roar."

"Nice to meet you, Roar. I'm Judah and this is Eli, my little brother."

"Sorry, we thought you were going to eat us with your large teeth," said Eli.

"I don't eat little boys with my teeth," said Roar.

"Eli, did you know that Tyrannosaurus Rex means Tyrant Lizard?"

"Really? That's funny Judah. The only thing I know is that they are carnivores," said Eli.

"Roar, this is Diamond the Brontosaurus," said Judah, introducing the two dinosaurs.

"Nice to meet you," said Roar

"Eli, you need to pronounce Tyrannosaurus Rex, tye-RAN-uh-SAW-us-REX," said Judah.

Eli giggled, "I'm sorry Roar. I didn't mean to mispronounce your name."

"That's okay Eli, you're still young," said Roar.

POP! They turned to see a Velociraptor GROWING, GROWING, GROWING! out of the toys.

Eli yelled, "YIKES! DINOSAURS ARE TAKING OVER THE BACKYARD!"

"THOSE FEET HAVE SHARP CLAWS!" SAID ELI.

"Oh no Eli! Mom will not like this. Velociraptors are very smart and fast. What if it eats us and gets out of the backyard to hunt for food?" said Judah.

"How do you know it will do that Judah? It could be a vegetarian like Diamond the Brontosaurus."

"Because Eli, look at those claws. They're like knives. Plus, there is a 99.9% chance that it's not," said Judah.

"I'm going to go find out." Eli yelled, "Hi dino! What's your name?"

"Eli! What are you doing? He's going to eat us," said Judah.

The Velociraptor looked at them. "I'm Joe and you are?"

"Nice to meet you, Joe. I'm Judah and this is Eli, my little brother."

"Sorry, we thought you were going to scratch us with your razor-like claws," said Eli.

"I don't scratch little boys with my claws," said Joe.

"Eli, did you know that Velociraptor means Quick Plunderer or Rapid Robber?"

"Really. That's funny Judah. The only thing I know is they are carnivores," said Eli.

"Joe, let us introduce you to the others. This is Diamond the Brontosaurus and Roar the Tyrannosaurus Rex," said Judah.

"Nice to meet you all," said Joe

"Eli, you need to pronounce Velociraptor, veh-loss-ih-RAP-tor," said Judah.

Eli giggled, "I'm sorry Joe. I didn't mean to mispronounce your name."

"That's okay Eli, you're still young," said Joe

SMACK! They turned to see a Pterodactyl **GROWING, GROWING, GROWING!** out of the toys.

Eli yelled, **"YIKES! DINOSAURS ARE TAKING OVER THE BACKYARD!"**

"LOOK AT THE FINGERS ON THOSE WINGS!" SAID ELI

"Oh no Eli! Mom will not like this. A Pterodactyl can fly. Who knows what kind of trouble it will get into if it leaves the backyard?" said Judah.

"We will ask it not to fly away," said Eli. Then he yelled, "Hi dino! What's your name?"

Flapping its wings, the Pterodactyl flew in the air, making a big circle around the other dinosaurs. It landed on top of the swing set.

"My name is Rapwing. I heard you boys talking and I won't fly out of the yard. I only weigh 10 pounds. I can't do much to get into trouble."

"Nice to meet you, Rapwing. I'm Judah and this is Eli, my little brother."

"Sorry, we thought you were going to carry us away with the pointy fingers on your wings," said Eli.

"I don't carry little boys away with my wings," said Rapwing. "Eli, did you know that Pterodactyl means Winged Finger?"

"Really? That's funny Judah. The only thing I know is they are carnivores," said Eli. "Rapwing, let us introduce you to the others. This is Diamond the Brontosaurus, Roar the Tyrannosaurus Rex, and Joe the Velociraptor," said Judah.

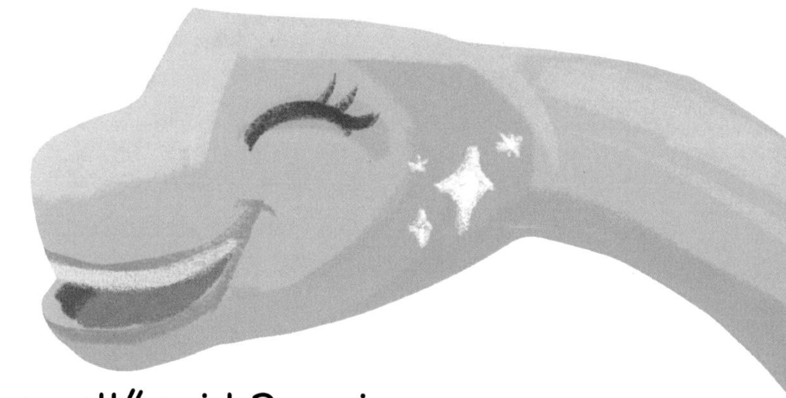

"Nice to meet you all," said Rapwing

"Eli, you need to pronounce Pterodactyl, TERR-uh-DAK-tuhl," said Judah.

Eli giggled, "I'm sorry Rapwing. I didn't mean to mispronounce your name."

"That's okay Eli, you're still young," said Rapwing

BURST! They turned to see a **STEGOSAURUS GROWING, GROWING, GROWING! OUT OF THE TOYS.** out of the toys.

Eli yelled, **"YIKES! DINOSAURS ARE TAKING OVER THE BACKYARD!"**

"THAT IS A BIG SPIKED TAIL!" SAID ELI.

"Oh no Eli! Mom will not like this. A Stegosaurus can cause a lot of damage with their tail. What if it knocks down all of the trees in the backyard?" said Judah.

"We keep thinking something bad is going to happen every time we see a new dinosaur, but it hasn't yet." Eli yelled, "Hi dino! What's your name?"

The small headed dinosaur smashed its big tail on the ground. The large plates on its back rippled, making the boys almost fall down.

"My name is Chomp."

"Nice to meet you, Chomp. I'm Judah and this is Eli, my little brother."

"Sorry, we thought you were going to crush us with your sharp tail," said Eli.

"I don't crush little boys with my tail," said Chomp.

"Eli, did you know that Stegosaurus means Roof Lizard?"

"Really? That's funny Judah. The only thing I know is they are herbivores," said Eli.

"Chomp, let us introduce you to the others. This is Diamond the Brontosaurus, Roar the Tyrannosaurus Rex, Joe the Velociraptor, and Rapwing the Pterodactyl," said Judah.

"Nice to meet you all," said Chomp. "Eli, you need to pronounce Stegosaurus, STEG-uh-SAWR-us," said Judah

Eli giggled, "I'm sorry Chomp. I didn't mean to mispronounce your name."

"That's okay Eli, you're still young," said Chomp

SNAP!

They turned to see the Triceratops **GROWING, GROWING, GROWING!!!** Out of the toys.

Eli yelled, "YIKES! THE DINOSAURS ARE TAKING OVER THE BACKYARD!!!!"

"THOSE ARE BIG HORNS!" SAID ELI.

"Oh no Eli. Mom will not like this. Can you imagine the amount of things a Triceratops could break with those three big horns?" said Judah.
"I think it's going to be really nice, just like our other dinosaurs." Eli yelled, "Hi dino! What's your name?"
Its head swung close to them. The Triceratops' big horns bumped into the deck, making it shake against the boys backs.
"Hello there, my name is Trihorn."
"Nice to meet you, Trihorn. I'm Judah and this is Eli, my little brother."
"Sorry, we thought you were going to knock us down with your three big horns," said Eli.

"I don't knock down little boys with my horns," said Trihorn.

"Eli, did you know that Triceratops means Three-horned Face?"

"Really? That's funny Judah. The only thing I know is they are herbivores," said Eli.

"Trihorn, let us introduce you to the others. This is Diamond the Brontosaurus, Roar the Tyrannosaurus Rex, Joe the Velociraptor, Rapwing the Pterodactyl, and Chomp the Stegosaurus," said Judah.

"Nice to meet you all," said Trihorn.

"Eli, you need to pronounce Triceratops, try-SAIR-uh-tops." said Judah.
Eli giggled, "I'm sorry Trihorn, I didn't mean to mispronounce your name."
"That's okay Eli, you're still young," said Trihorn

CRACK! They looked to see an Ankylosaurus **GROWING, GROWING, GROWING!** out of the toys.

Eli yelled, **"YIKES! DINOSAURS ARE TAKING OVER THE BACKYARD!"**

said Eli.

"Oh no Eli! Mom will not like this. That looks like a turtle with spikes on it, but it's not. What if it gets in the pond and destroys everything?" said Judah.

"We don't know it will do that, Judah." Eli yelled, "Hi dino! What's your name?"

"Hi," the Ankylosaurus said in a shy, quiet voice, as it rested its large, clubbed tail on the ground. "My name is Bumpy."

"Nice to meet you, Bumpy. I'm Judah and this is Eli, my little brother."

"Sorry, we thought you were going to hurt us with your armor-like spikes," said Eli.

"I don't hurt little boys with my spikes," said Bumpy.

"Eli, did you know that Ankylosaurus means Fused Lizard?"

"Really. That's funny Judah. The only thing I know is they are herbivores," said Eli.

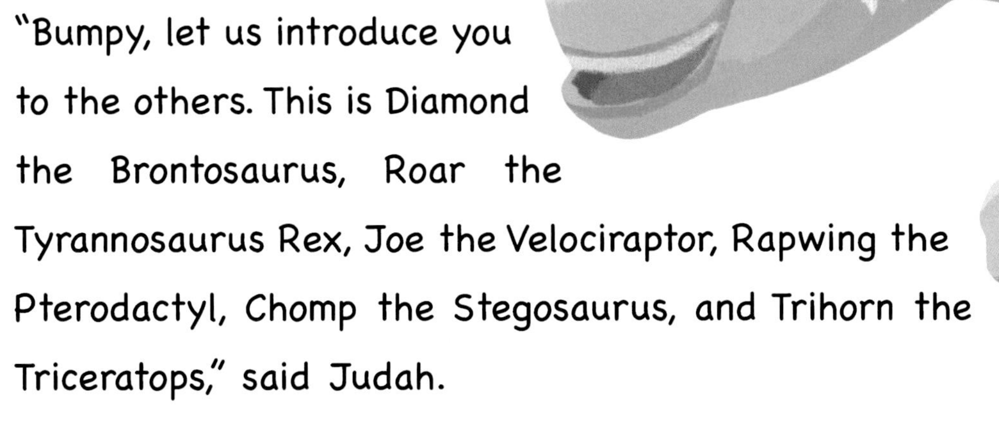

"Bumpy, let us introduce you to the others. This is Diamond the Brontosaurus, Roar the Tyrannosaurus Rex, Joe the Velociraptor, Rapwing the Pterodactyl, Chomp the Stegosaurus, and Trihorn the Triceratops," said Judah.

"Nice to meet you all," whispered Bumpy.

"Eli, you need to pronounce Ankylosaurus ang-KILE-uh-SAWR-us," said Judah

Eli giggled, "I'm sorry Bumpy, I didn't mean to mispronounce your name."

"That's okay Eli, you're still young," said Bumpy

SPLIT! They turned to see a Parasaurolophus **GROWING, GROWING, GROWING!** out of the toys.

ELI YELLED, "YIKES! DINOSAURS ARE TAKING OVER THE BACKYARD!"

"Oh no Eli, Mom will not like this. We're running out of room. We're going to have to stand under the dinosaurs if they don't stop growing," said Judah.

"We can just get on top of them!" Diamond lifted them up into the air. Eli yelled, "Hi dino! What's your name?"

"Hello there, young men," she yelled up to them. "My name is Venus."

Judah yelled down at her. "Nice to meet you, Venus. I'm Judah and this is Eli, my little brother."

"Sorry, we thought you were going to hit us with your longhorn or step on us because we are running out of room on the ground," said Eli.

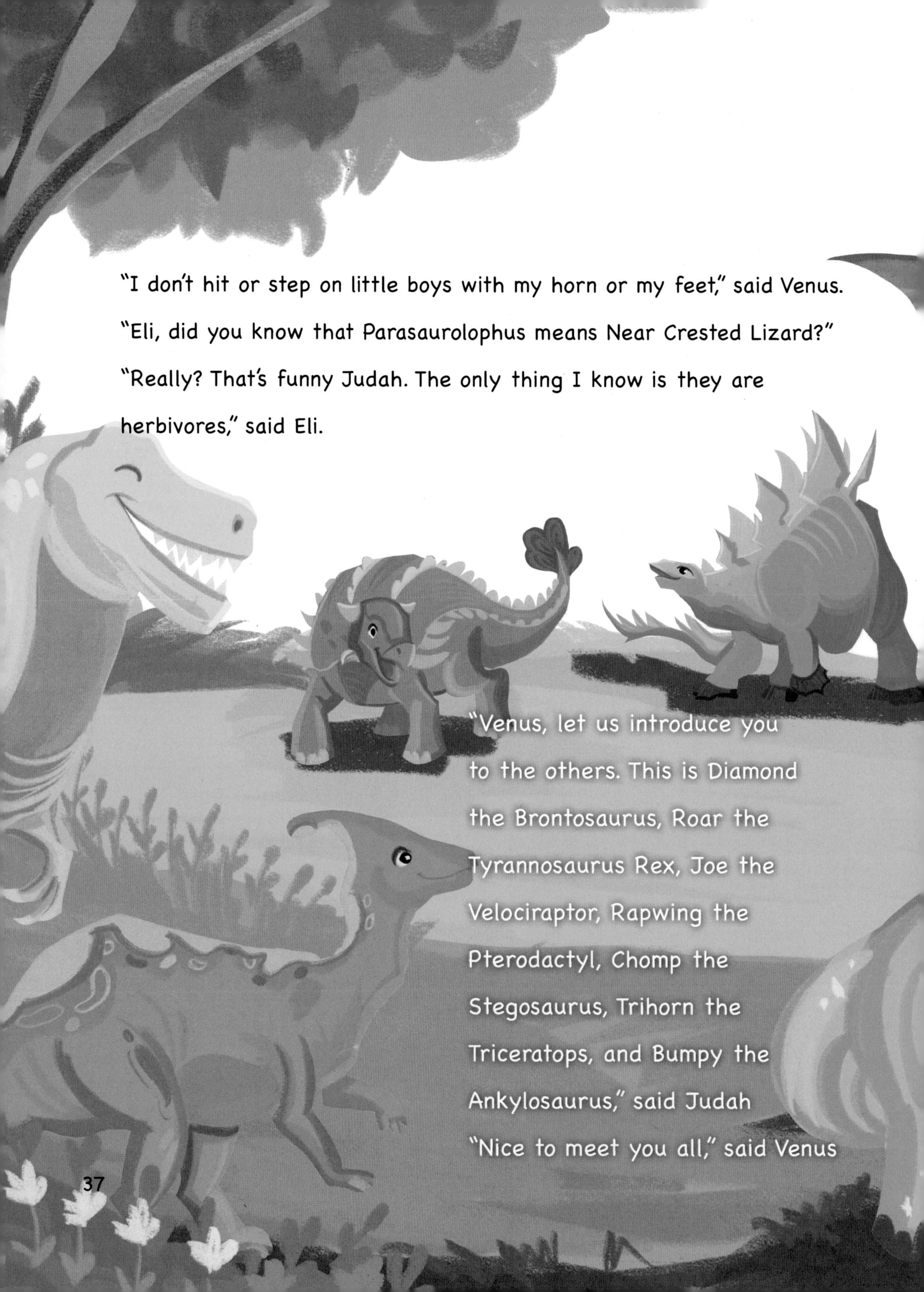

"I don't hit or step on little boys with my horn or my feet," said Venus. "Eli, did you know that Parasaurolophus means Near Crested Lizard?"

"Really? That's funny Judah. The only thing I know is they are herbivores," said Eli.

"Venus, let us introduce you to the others. This is Diamond the Brontosaurus, Roar the Tyrannosaurus Rex, Joe the Velociraptor, Rapwing the Pterodactyl, Chomp the Stegosaurus, Trihorn the Triceratops, and Bumpy the Ankylosaurus," said Judah

"Nice to meet you all," said Venus

"Eli, you need to pronounce Parasaurolophus, par-ah-SAWR-OL-uh-fus," said Judah.

Eli giggled, "I'm sorry Venus, I didn't mean to mispronounce your name."

"That's okay Eli, you're still young," said Venus

BOOM! They turned to see their Mom coming, Coming, COMING! out the out the back door.

Eli yelled, **"YIKES! MOM IS TAKING OVER THE BACKYARD!"**

"JUDAH AND ELIAS, GET DOWN OFF THE TOP OF THE SWING SET RIGHT NOW!" said their Mom.

Eli yelled, "Mom! Dinosaurs are taking over the backyard! Would you like to meet them?" he said, as he held out the dino for her to see.

"I would love to meet your dinosaurs when you're both sitting at the table and are ready for dinner," said their Mom.

"Okay!" said Judah, jumping off the swing set.

Eli dropped his dino on the ground. Then he hopped down by himself.

"Come on boys, your little sister is hungry."

The boys played peek-a-boo with baby Eden in her high chair while their Mom got dinner ready.

THUMP! They turned and heard their Dad **WALKING DOWN THE STEPS.**

Eli yelled, "YIKES! DINOSAURS ARE TAKING OVER THE HOUSE NOW!"

"No Eli, that's just Dad walking down the stairs." Judah smiled as his Dad walked into the kitchen to join the family for dinner.

Eli giggled and gave his little sister a kiss as his mother sat down plates in front of each of them.

Judah looked at Eli and laughed. "I wonder if the race cars will take over the driveway tomorrow?"
Eli started laughing, too. So hard, in fact, that peas shot out of his nose, sending the entire family into hysterical laughter. Even the baby giggled.

THE END

Fun things to know about Dinosaurs

The Brontosaurus had nose holes on the top of its head.
The Tyrannosaurus Rex has only been found to have lived in the United States and Canada.
The Velociraptor may have had feathers like the birds we see today.
The Pterodactyl was around 3.5 feet long and has only been found in Africa and Europe.
The Stegosaurus had a brain the size of a walnut.
The Triceratops had a beak like a bird for its mouth and is the state dinosaur of Wyoming.
The Ankylosaurus had a club for a tail to defend itself. It could be swung around to hit things.
The Parasaurolophus had rows of hundreds of teeth. When they would wear down, new ones would take their place.

The facts about the Dinos in this book were learned from:
https://www.factsjustforkids.com/dinosaur-facts

About the Author

Deana lives in Knoxville, TN with her husband and small dog. She is the author of "A Parent's Guide To Navigating Child Care," released in the fall of 2020. Deana started 2021 by writing the children's book, "Lucy's Lost in the Everglades", with the intention to educate children about snakes. She is also the author of "Oh My Sweet Lidy," "Octavia Gets Her Veiled Chameleon" and "Barry's Smoky Mountain Adventure." She is currently working on other books and hopes to release them over the next few years.

Closing Bible Verse

"For we live by faith, not by sight."
2 Corinthians 5:7

About the Illustrator

Darlee, also known as Happylee, is a multi-disciplinary Filipino creative, based in the Philippines. She is an art extraordinaire who is proficient in digital illustrations, painting, calligraphy, graphic design, and traditional art. She believes that art is an extension of herself and soul. She continuously strives to learn new things and endeavors to keep improving her works. By creating magical and whimsical inspired pieces, she creates happiness for herself and hopes to impart this happiness to the viewer as well. She is an old soul and a family oriented person. When she is not creating art she enjoys a good cup of coffee, books, good movies, tv shows, anime and singing.

To reach Happylee and find out more about her, visit:

www.thehappylee.com

Oh My
Sweet
Lidy
Written by
Deana Charcalla
Illustrated by
Carmalitta Barbour

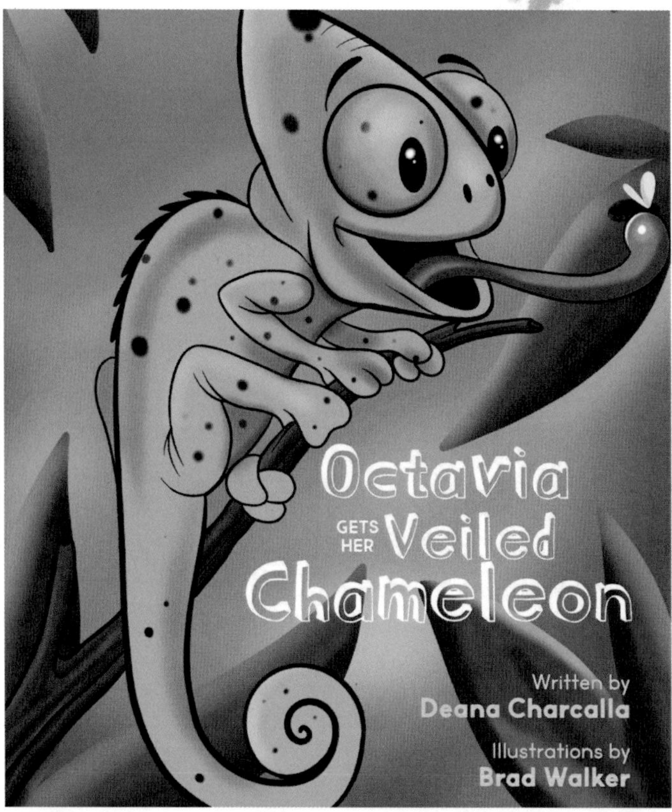
Octavia
GETS HER Veiled
Chameleon
Written by
Deana Charcalla
Illustrations by
Brad Walker

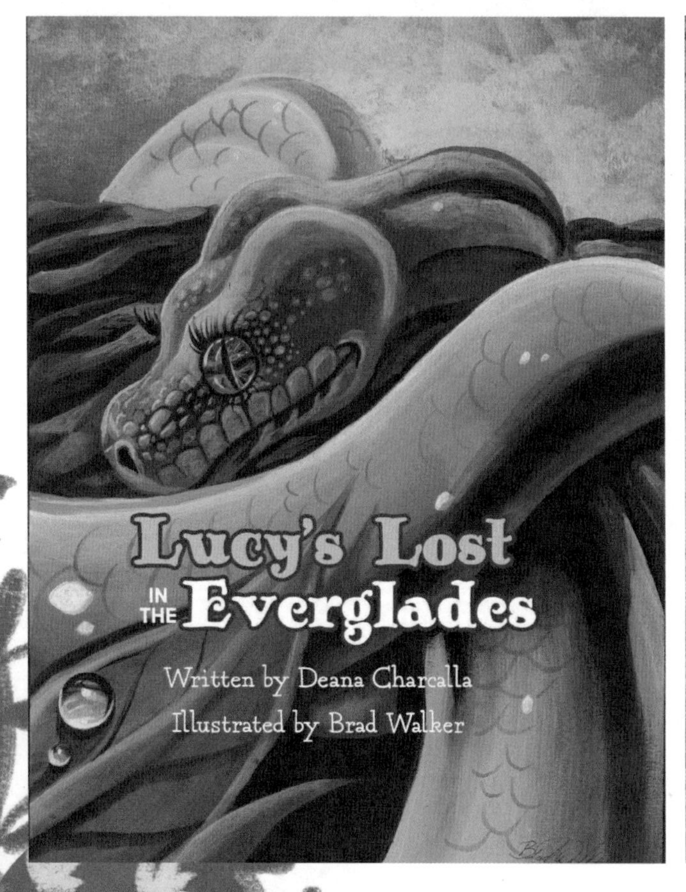
Lucy's Lost
IN THE Everglades
Written by Deana Charcalla
Illustrated by Brad Walker

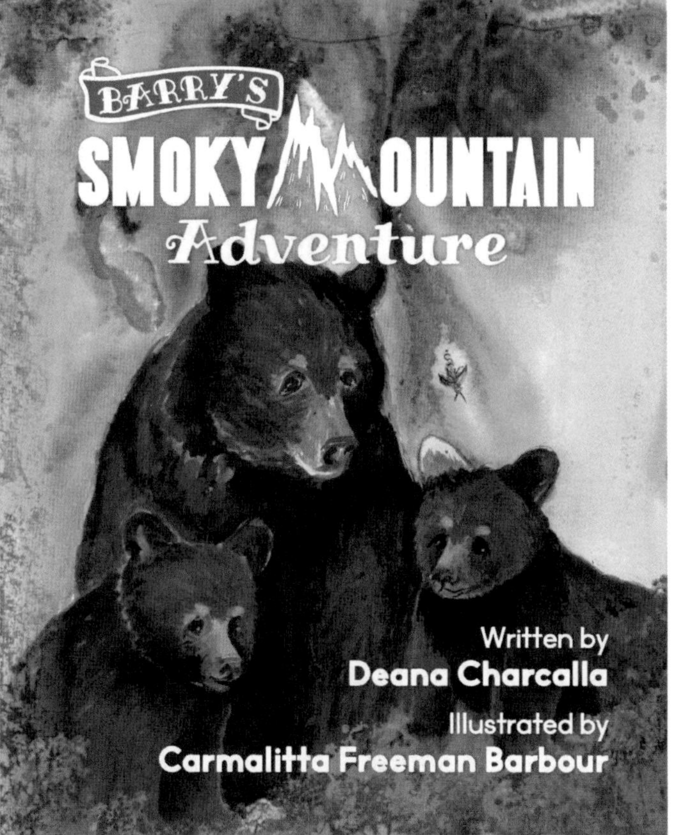
BARRY'S
SMOKY MOUNTAIN
Adventure
Written by
Deana Charcalla
Illustrated by
Carmalitta Freeman Barbour

DeanaBean.com

CHARACTERS NAMED BY

GAVIN RANSDEL

age 6
Chomp the Stegosaurus

JUDAH AKERS

age 4
Venus the Parasaurolophus

MILES ROBB

age 8
Rapwing the Pterodactyl

Ava Akers

age 10
Diamond
the Brontosaurus

Avery Akers

age 12
Roar the Tyrannosaurus Rex

Sammy Robb

age 5
Trihorn the Triceratops

Made in the USA
Middletown, DE
21 November 2022